A TEMPLAR BOOK

First published in the UK in 2020 by Templar Publishing,
an imprint of Bonnier Books UK,
The Plaza, 535 King's Road, London, SW10 0SZ
www.templarco.co.uk
www.bonnierpublishing.com

Text and illustrations copyright © 2020 by Sam Usher
Design copyright © 2020 by Templar Books

1 3 5 7 9 10 8 6 4 2

ISBN 978-1-78741-742-7 (Hardback)
ISBN 978-1-78741-685-7 (Paperback)

Designed by Genevieve Webster
Edited by Alison Ritchie

Printed in China

FSC
www.fsc.org
MIX
Paper from
responsible sources
FSC® C104723

This book belongs to:

....

Sam Usher

WILD

templar
books

When I woke up
this morning,
it was looking-after-
the-cat day.

Grandad said,
"They'll be here any minute!"

And I said,
"All we have to do is play with her,
feed her, and cuddle her!
Easy!"

We said hello.

And first we tried
playing with her.

But did she
want to play?

NO!

I said, "Grandad, I don't think she likes me."
And he said, "It's okay, cats have a mind of their own.
Why don't we try feeding her?"

So we tried to feed her.

But was she hungry?

NO!

I said, "Grandad, she won't eat
ANYTHING.
She definitely doesn't like me!"

And Grandad said, "It's okay, you can't make a cat
do anything it doesn't want to.
Let's see if she wants a nap and a cuddle
in front of the fire."

So we made up a fire.
But did she want a nap and a cuddle?

NO!

She did NOT!

I said,
"Grandad! Quick! The cat's gone wild.
She's escaped!"

There wasn't a moment to lose!

I said, "This way, Grandad . . ."

And there she
was.

We tried to
follow her.

And got lost along
the way.

But then we found her again!

She led us to her friends.
And we joined in their
wild party.

Back at home,
Grandad said,
"Well, you never
know what surprises
wild creatures
have in store!"

And I agreed.
I said, "Look, Grandad,
she likes me now!
Can she come and
stay again tomorrow?"

Also by Sam Usher:

ISBN: 978-1-78370-547-4

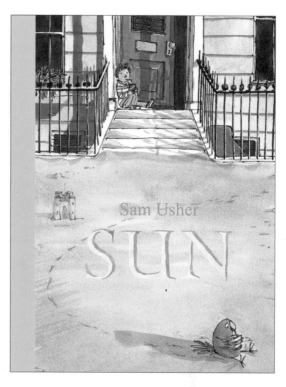

ISBN: 978-1-78370-795-9

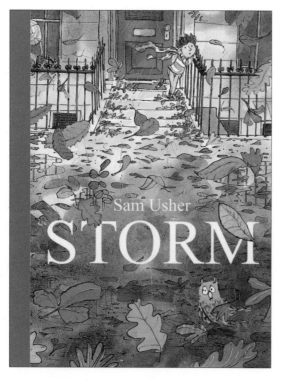

ISBN: 978-1-78741-242-2

ISBN: 978-1-78370-073-8